Walking the Cat

Story by Pat Harrison
Pictures by Valerie Romanow

Mom said, "Here you are, Mike.

Where is Fluffy?"

Mike went to look for Fluffy.

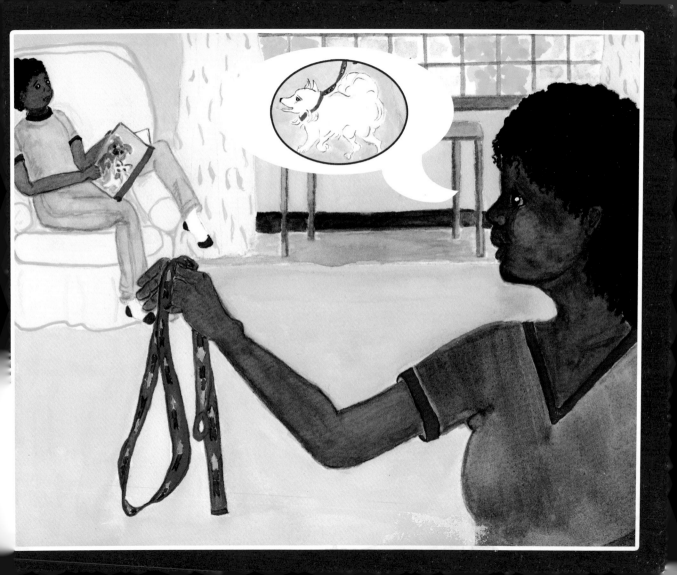

"Come on, Fluffy," said Mike.

"We are going for a walk."

Tim said,

"Here comes Mike and Fluffy."

Mike said,

"Go and get your cat, Tim!

We can go

for a walk."

Tim went to get the cat.

"Come here, Kitty," said Tim.

The cat ran and Tim ran too.

"Go Tim, go!" shouted Jen.

"Come on," said Tim.

"Come for a walk, Kitty."

"**Meoooow**!" said Kitty.

"Come up here, Kitty.

We can go for a walk

like this," said Tim.

Tim and Mike went for a walk.

Jen went home and said,

"Mom, can I get a cat?"

ALBERT'S
Impossible
Toothache

Barbara Williams

illustrated by Doug Cushman

WALKER BOOKS
AND SUBSIDIARIES
LONDON • BOSTON • SYDNEY

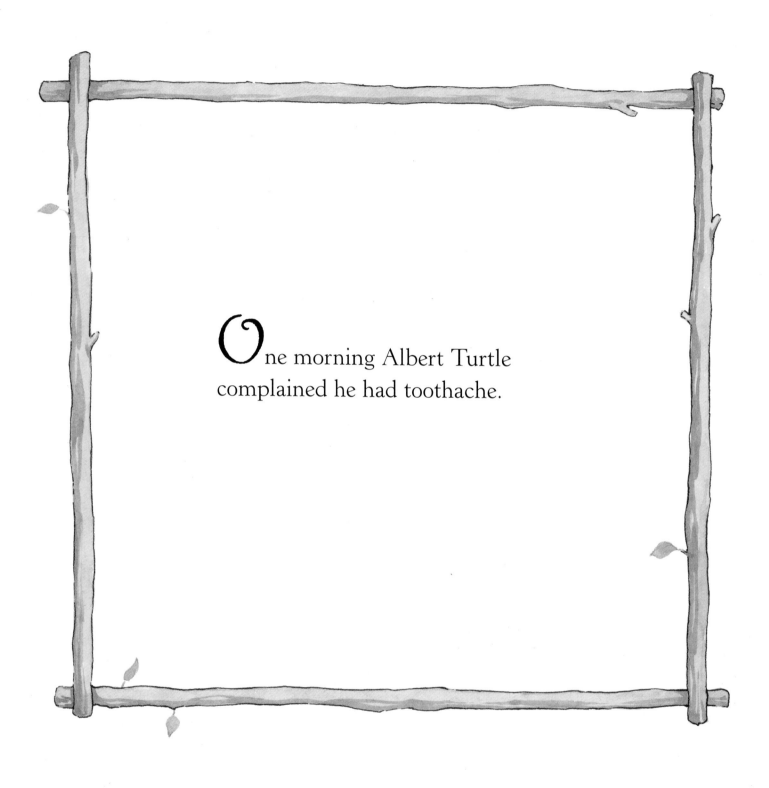

One morning Albert Turtle
complained he had toothache.

"Who ever heard of a turtle with toothache?" said Albert's sister, Marybelle.

All the same, Albert was sure he had toothache and needed to stay in bed.

"See," said Albert's father, pointing to his own toothless mouth. "I don't have toothache. And Homer doesn't have toothache. And Marybelle doesn't have toothache. And your mother doesn't have toothache. It's impossible for anyone in our family to have toothache."

"You never believe me," said Albert.

"I'd believe you if you told the truth," said Albert's father.

"You believed Homer when he said he didn't break the window," Albert reminded his father.

"I'm worried about Albert," said Albert's mother at breakfast.

"You *should* be worried about a boy who doesn't tell the truth," said Albert's father as he left for work.

"Albert just doesn't want to eat his black ants," said Marybelle.

"If I had toothache, I'd still want to eat my black ants," announced Homer.

"Come and eat your black ants, Albert," called his mother.

But Albert just moaned softly from the bedroom.

Albert's mother kissed Homer and Marybelle goodbye and sat down in her worrying chair.

She worried and worried.

Then she had an idea.

"Look," she said to Albert. "I've made you a special breakfast of all your favourite things – dandelion leaves sprinkled with blackberries, a fat slug and half a juicy earthworm."

"I can't eat anything," said Albert. "I have toothache."

"Of course you don't have toothache," said his mother.

"You never believe me," said Albert.

"I'd believe you if you told the truth," said Albert's mother.

"You believed Dad when he said he'd caught a seven-pound trout," Albert reminded her.

Albert's mother took the tray back to the kitchen and
went outside to her worrying swing.
She worried and worried.

Then she had another idea.
"Come out and play catch with me," she said.

"I can't play catch with you," said Albert.
"I have toothache."
"You just think you have toothache,"
said Albert's mother.
"You never believe me," whined Albert.
"You believed Marybelle when she said she
was the only girl in her class who wasn't
allowed to go to a birthday sleepover on a
school night."

Albert's mother put the ball away and went outside to her worrying rock in the sun.
She worried and worried.

Then she had a new idea.

"Look, Albert, I've brought the photo album to show you the pictures we took in Disneyland. Sit up, Albert."

"I can't sit up," said Albert. "Why don't you ever believe me?"

Albert's mother put the photo album away and went into the sitting-room to lie down on her worrying sofa.

She worried and worried.

She was still worrying when Marybelle and Homer came home.

"How's Albert?" asked Marybelle.

"He still says he has toothache," said Albert's mother.

"He just didn't want to fight Dilworth Dunlap," explained Marybelle. "He was waiting for Albert after school."

"If I had toothache, I'd still fight Dilworth Dunlap," announced Homer.

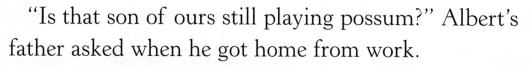

"Is that son of ours still playing possum?" Albert's father asked when he got home from work.

"Yes," said Albert's mother. "I wish he would remember he's a turtle."

"He just knew we were having cricket legs for dinner," said Marybelle.

"I don't want any cricket legs either," said Homer.

After dinner Grandmother Turtle came over with jelly worms for all the children.

"Can I have Albert's?" asked Marybelle. "He won't want it. He says he has toothache."

"Isn't that awful?" said Albert's mother.

"Can you believe your grandson would say an impossible thing like that?" asked Albert's father.

"The trouble with all of you is that you never believe him," said Albert's grandmother.

Albert's grandmother went into his bedroom.
"Well," she said. "I hear you have toothache."
"Yes," said Albert.
"*Where* do you have toothache?" asked Albert's grandmother.

"In my left toe," said Albert. "A mouse bit me when I stepped in his hole."

"Well, I have just the thing to fix toothache," said Albert's grandmother. She took her handkerchief out of her bag and wrapped it round Albert's toe.

Albert smiled toothlessly and got out of bed.

For Kim
B. W.

To my expat writing friends and dinner companions in Paris –
Liberté, Egalité, Fromager!
D. C.

First published 2003 by Walker Books Ltd
87 Vauxhall Walk, London SE11 5HJ

2 4 6 8 10 9 7 5 3 1

Text © 2003 Barbara Williams
Illustrations © 2003 Doug Cushman

The right of Barbara Williams and Doug Cushman to be identified
as author and illustrator respectively of this work has been asserted by them
in accordance with the Copyright, Designs and Patents Act 1988

This book has been typeset in Horley

Printed in Italy

British Library Cataloguing in Publication Data:
a catalogue record for this book
is available from the British Library

ISBN 0-7445-8598-8